The sun and the moon

Rigby®

A Harcourt Achieve Imprint

www.Rigby.com
1-800-531-5015

The sun is going down.

The birds go to sleep.

I go to bed.

I go to sleep.

The moon is up.

8

I sleep,

and I sleep,

and I sleep.

The sun is up.

13

The birds are up.

15

I am up.